# Mine!

Written by
## Sarah Hammond

Illustrated by
## Laura Hughes

# PaRragon

Bath · New York · Cologne · Melbourne · Delhi
Hong Kong · Shenzhen · Singapore · Amsterdam

Kitty is in her bedroom.
Today, she is a waitress.

Kitty sets out her things
—the pasta on the plates
and the cookies in the bowls,
the cups on the saucers with the teapot
and the milk and the spoons.

# The diner is open!
## Here come the customers!

Tea for Teddy in the tall cup.
Cake for Pansy on the pink plate.
Cookies for Bingo in the brown bowl.

kitty's diner

**Knock, knock**
on the diner door.

**Who could it be?**

**"Look, Kitty,"** says Mommy, **"Leah has come
to play and she's brought some chocolate cakes.
Can she be a waitress too?"**

**"Let's take turns,"** says Kitty.
**"You can be my helper first, Leah!"**

"I know!" shouts Leah.
"Let's have some music!

We can all dance."

"**Not like that!**"
says Kitty.
"And you're in
**Teddy's** seat!"

**"I know!"** shouts Leah.
"Let's have a contest!"
She makes a tower of cookies
and balances them on her head.

**"Look, Kitty! No hands!"**
"Not like that!" says Kitty.
"Cookies go in the **brown bowl!**"

"I know!" shouts Leah.
"The diner needs some new customers!"
She gets Rooster and Penny Polly.

"Come on, animals—lunch time!"

"Not like that!" says Kitty.
"The animals live on the farm!"

**"My turn to be the waitress now!"** sings Leah.

**"No! This diner is MINE!"**
shouts Kitty, and she hides the teapot in her tent.

And the plates,

bowls,

spoons,

milk,

cakes,

the pasta, the cookies,
the cups and the saucers, and
Teddy, and Pansy, and Bingo.

**"The diner is closed!"**

Inside the tent, it is dark.
Teddy is quiet.
Pansy goes to sleep. Bingo is still.
They don't want tea or cake
or cookies anymore.

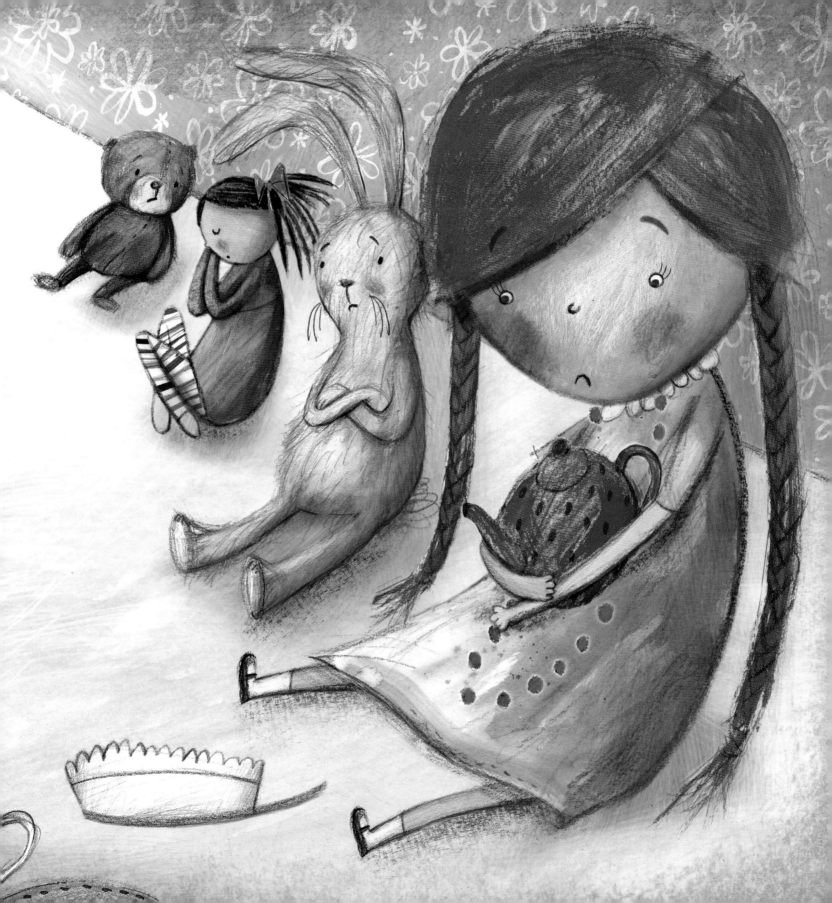

**Knock, knock,**
on the tent door.
"It's raining out here,"
says Leah.
"Can we come in?"

Kitty cuddles Teddy up close. Now there
is room for Leah and the animals too.
Teddy smiles. Pansy wakes up.
Bingo is hungry again.

"I know!" shouts Kitty.
"Let's have an inside picnic!"

"Yesssss!!!"
says Leah.

Tea for Teddy in the tall cup.
Cake for Pansy on the pink plate.
Cookies for Bingo in the brown bowl...

kitty +
leah's den

with
music...

and
dancing...

a balancing
contest...

**and chocolate cakes
for Leah and Kitty to share.**

**For Charlotte**

S.H.

**For Anthony**

L.H.

This edition published by Parragon Books Ltd in 2014
and distributed by

Parragon Inc.
440 Park Avenue South, 13th Floor
New York, NY 10016
www.parragon.com

Published by arrangement with Meadowside Children's Books

Text © Sarah Hammond 2013
Illustrations © Laura Hughes 2013

ISBN 978-1-4723-3423-7

Printed in China